To YAHWEH,

undefeated king of the breezes,

giver of life,

who seeps—

much of this was written January/February 2025
while studying
Hebrew Bible and ancient civilizations
at Collège de France
while staying in an apartment built
into the 12th century wall
in Paris' 5th arrondissement
steps from where Joyce & Hemingway wrote
their tales

the layers of time,
where humanity continues on...

NAKED LITTLE FICTIONS
2029

BRIAN J. SHIRCLIFF

Naked Little Fictions: 2029

ISBN: 978-1-954688-34-6

0101110110 3 0101000 2
2 0001111 232
0000000111110001

two voices, whispers interrupting

"My dear faculty and staff, it is my pleasure to stand before you in my position as Vice Chairman of this very school's Board of Trustees. Indeed, I look forward to rising to be your Chairman next year. And on this pivotal day I stand before you to express my personal support for Father President's important announcement today. Some of you taught me, I am proud to say, and some of you are teaching my son—my son Harold. Though you, um, you probably know he's going by Aro these, uh, these, these days. The young man—young person, person—with the, um, the hair. Yes. Yes. He is, he's, he's my son, Aro is my son. Well, for those of you I haven't had the pleasure of meeting, I'm Charles Harold Oden IV. The Chair—uh Father—Father asked me to be here today as a close personal friend of his, of Father Bob, um, of Father President, as he announces the, uh, the unilateral decision he has made that our bylaws—at least we think—that our bylaws permit him to do with the powers of his office as Chief Executive Officer of our

          Naked Little Fictions: 2029

dear school, our beloved alma mater with 101 years of history behind it. So, with no further ado, as I exit the podium here, I ask whoever it is back there to please begin the livestream transmission of this important announcement to the whole world with us gathered here, with me as the sole representative of the Board in attendance and our dear faculty and staff."

"We go live on my count. Three. Two. One. My dear friends, I give you myself: Father President Robert Moresley of this fine institution—Saint Thomas Aquinas College Preparatory here in downtown Cincinnati, OH—where we are all gathered today for my very special announcement to our Board and to our Saint Thomas Aquinas faculty & staff. Last night thanks to the brutally honest and courageous confession of our very own President of the United States of America we learned just how powerful holograms can be. What seems like simple light and sound—all those intricate ones and zeroes behind them—generate our very reality, can even stand in as reality. After all, I posit the important question—no the important realization—"what is real?" Holograms and AI responses inserted into the mouths of those holograms can be as real as anything, real enough that even a bitter opponent standing nearby could not even notice the difference—"

      "—or got paid off to play right along—"

"—would you, would you please have the courtesy to save your commentary for the faculty lunchroom?

This is live. LIVE—I tell you. I cannot and will not take any commentary from a wo—oh dear—oh dear me—no, no, no—I'm getting carried away—taken off track by this this this vul—this vulv—oh dear me—oh dear—we, we can take this piece out of the final, yes. I'm okay here. It's okay, it's all okay—now, now where was I—damn it—God damn it—vile, vile woman—<u>woman</u>—where was—where was I—oh yes, yes, the big announcement—

I have taken bold action of investing our entire scholarship endowment and our faculty's retirement savings into a new venture that promises to double our future each year. Perhaps even every two months by our bravest expert calculation. Yes. You heard that right. DOUBLE OUR FUTURE. Can you imagine what is possible with such a risk? Such a bold move...a wise and calculated gamble some would say."

"—will our retirement accounts double as well?"

"Now, now, good sir, you'll get what's owed to you. You see, the more important question to ask is 'What is it?' or even better 'What goodness are you unleashing upon the Earth, Father President Moresley?' Well, let me first give you a few hints. Ah yes. My list. At the very top: It will encourage our young people to mature at a faster rate and without the dreadful fear of pre-marital pregnancy for those of us fiercely Catholic and most concerned with life. It will preserve vocations — St. Dominic, pray for us!

St. Thomas Aquinas, pray for us! You know you all are to say these with me to be good Christian examples for our children and the world. Now, after me... St. Dominic—! God damn it! I warn—I remind—I remind you as President of our glorious school— God damn it—God damn it—oh me—oh dear me— what—what was it—what was it I was saying—

my list, next—and—and—and our new venture will save all those failing marriages as we have tipped well past the 50% divorce rate among faculty at this Christ-centered Catholic school these last two years, even when including only first marriages. At our beloved, very dear <u>Catholic</u> institution! I mean look at you, so many of you now divorced, some of you divorced for the second time—God help you— all of you promising before our Good God that you'd remain in wedlock for the rest of your lives. Ten years ago you would've never gotten away with that here, but as vocations to teaching have dwindled, well, what am I to do. Dear, dear, dear friends. You must be incredibly grateful we don't enforce canon law here. You'd be fired. I should fire you as your loving President, as the loving thing to do, to correct you. I should enforce upon you our dearest and wisest canon law—for your own good and the good example for our students. If you don't rise to the pinnacle—the priesthood—as I have courageously followed that call, then you <u>must</u> marry and have children. Many children. That's what you are to be doing. None of this birth control. None of this deciding when to have kids—<u>or if</u>—God help you...!

Marry. Procreate. Do your duty to God and church and country. It's natural law. Not mine. God's law, holy law, upon which our Pure and Holy Mother Church is founded and bolstered through the ever pure logic of our school's namesake. St. Thomas Aquinas, pray for us! I have the courage and bold faith to ask him to do so, to ask my brother Aquinas to pray for you and me. And you should too, God damn it! Our Holy Mother Church: pure without the foul sex trying to lead. Our Holy Mother Church: cared for by holy celibate men like myself who have advanced—and will advance further—with bold leadership like my own—our church and my ever-rising position within it. St. Dominic, pray for _me_!"

"—when do we get to the part of the story
when he falls on his sword—"

"I'd like to remind you that you are risking the fires of hell. Each one of you who speaks out, out of turn, each of you whispering out there like vile snakes, accursed snakes. Each and every one of you divorced or even considering divorce. Each and every one of you single people. Many of you masquerade as single when in fact I see you on the dating apps, see you selling your future for a hookup. God help us even more, sometimes hooking up with someone of the same sex. Dear..."

"—he just admitted he's on the dating apps—"<br>"—of course he is—he goes by **twinkreceiver**—"<br>"—celibate my ass—"

"And if you could read and speak Latin, the one true language that united all the Earth at one point, you'd know the riches of our law, our one true church, our Holy Mother—inscribed from God's mouth to St. Thomas Aquinas' gentle ears and through his fingers and onto parchment—the one true language, God's holy language, but alas, only a few of us here know Latin. Latin: the language of our Lord—Latin: the language we SHOULD be speaking at every Mass when we eat this bread and drink this cup—"

"—the whole Earth?—
what a small-minded moron—"
"—ummm, does this dumbass motherfucker know that Latin is the language spoken by Jesus' killers—"
"—and that Jesus likely never spoke a word of Latin—"

"Mysterium Fidei. Yes, you should say it now as you do in our very holy Latin Mass—the Tridentine Mass—every Wednesday where I lead you into the good graces of our dear God. But you probably do not know what it means. Mysterium Fidei. You don't know; but I do. And I am kind. I will help you. In our vulgar English it sounds so boring: 'The Mystery of Faith.' But not in Latin. Mysterium Fidei. Hear it roll so easily off my tongue? Say it with me. Say it loud. Say it with pride— the one true pride! Mysterium Fidei!!!!"

— silence, not even a breeze —
— not even the hum of the HVAC —

"I should fire you all. I should expose you to the Catholic press and let the zealous dogs have you, have their way with you—make up a bunch of terrible things to ruin your lives. But I do not. I exercise tremendous compassion. Even what you divulge in the most holy sacrament of Penance should get you fired—every sordid detail of your sinful desires and even better—even worse—even worse your concrete actions in lusting after each other. What you tell me in your confessions should be grounds for your dismissal. But I am gentle and kind—"

"—and a complete ass—"

"At your interview before I hired you, I should have asked you about your sex lives. I should have found out just how much you are doing your duty as good Catholics, as good Americans of the United States of America, in growing in holiness, in growing our ranks from the bottom—"

"—Jesus—"<br>"—he has the audacity
to talk to us about holiness—"<br>"—after last year!??—"

"If I did fire you...where would you go? Where would you—I mean. Really?! I am saving you—I want to help you here grieving your divorces—as you'll never be moral in the eyes of our one true Roman Catholic Church that has done only good things for fellow believers in Christ our Lord and Holy King—"

"—has he not heard
about the Albigensian Crusade —
let alone the other exceedingly brutal crusades—
the Pope's Albigensian Crusade burned alive
entire towns of Christians and Jews—
burned <u>alive</u>—men, women, and children—
to establish new papal-controlled lands
for the Roman Catholic Church
and French royalty
in areas that wanted nothing to do
with kings or popes—
the Catholic Church
and French royalty joined forces
to kill innocent people
and then followed up these genocides with the
even crueler Inquisition led by his own—"

"And those of you still in your marriages, I want to save you, save them, preserve the sanctity that our Lord Christ guarantees in our most blessed sacrament sealed by Christ's holy priest who married you all. Often <u>me</u>. You swore before me that you would be co-joined with our dear God by my sharing the sacrament of Holy Matrimony with you with all the power vested in me and my ever pure and exceedingly stylish vestments."

"—your vestments look more like Pontius Pilate
and the Roman aristocracy than someone
as prophetic as Jesus—"

"—or as homeless as Jesus—"

                                "—does he not know that
Jesus spurned that bloody mafia title of 'Christ'—
                 and all the royal nastiness that goes with it—"

                                       "—if you love Jesus
                 you would not call him Christ or Messiah,
                                        that's for damned sure!"

"Jealous of my fine vestments, are you? As I stand
here as Christ before you. Dear, dear sniveling
women. Jealousy is a terrible sin. Too bad the
Good Lord could never call you to the priesthood—
as such a lofty position is only available to men, to
those of us assigned the lofty title of 'male' at birth."

          "—did you not hear me?? You are dressed more
          like the killer of Jesus than a follower of Jesus!
                                       Wake the holy fuck up!"

              "If Jesus had a choice of eating and talking
          with you or a woman, whom would he choose?
                      In the gospels he always chooses
                 the least significant person of his time—"

              "—come on, man, Jesus was a person of love,
                              not a weapon to be wielded!"

"If my threats do not enliven your faith, my
announcement today will offer you all some hope—
about how I am investing your retirement savings
in something ingenious. In something that will save
you <u>and</u> make you rich all at once."

"—so you are guaranteeing more
in our retirement portfolios?"

"And—and—I suspect our investment will end mass shootings even without the need to take away our—your, your—guns. People will be happier, safer, more satisfied, more in charge, perhaps than we've ever been on this planet. Even though we are quite safe here on campus with our specially designed product, our Ch(e)cker System. You all know Ch(e)cker is the company we acquired last year within our ever-growing tech-portfolio. This very same system is used all over the country—even on our beloved city's Fountain Square where our students will safely lunch during the field trip today. Our students and everyone on the Square will be safe and sound...even when there will surely be protests about our dear President's innocent move to substitute a hologram of himself into the United States Presidential Debate so that he could attend his son's basketball game. We all surely understand, Mr. President. Don't we all? Hmm? Well, today, our students on Fountain Square will be as safe as anyone ever with that Ch(e)cker System, ever safer in the presence of our fellow God-fearing Religionists speaking God's hard-won truth to the Dumbsters—or whatever ridiculous name they are going by today."

"Does he really think Ch(e)cker
or his ridiculous vestments
would stop an attack?"

"But I'm not here today to tell you about all the incredible benefits of the Ch(e)cker System and how it scrambles signals and prevents drones from dropping weapons ordered online into any area Ch(e)cker tracks. Yes, even _that_ kind of safe. A true border. As much as I'd like to sing ever more Ch(e)cker's praises—you of course could find out more by checking it out with your favorite browser. And lingering there awhile.

No. I'm here to share the news about our _newest_ little invention.

Our little invention will soothe rage as well as it resolves lust.

Our little invention—well, I must be clear that we did not invent it but we are investing to expand it. Our invention—our investment, our _investment_. Yes. Must get this right for the lawyers—_investment_—

well—to set the stage for you to discern the importance of today's announcement—and to clear the air—_again_—first let me remind you all of something you might've forgotten, it was all so trivial. But telling you this will help you understand why I've done what I've done—not about _that_—but about our little invention—investment, _investment_.

As you might remember, my very personal algorithm was leaked last year. It was of course stolen from the megacomputers remembering everything you and I ever get even the least bit curious about on our devices—or at least <u>someone</u> got curious using my device and login as must have surely happened to me. And mine—my record of all the sites I've visited—was stolen and leaked to the world. I do wonder how much someone paid for that—to try to ruin me. I am worth far more than anyone realizes. But it didn't work. By the love of Christ, our champion, our warrior, our redeemer, our king, I continue to stand here as your dear Father President, pure and ever holy. What I have viewed—what someone viewed on my computer, day after day—well that should be my business and the business of my order within our wider Catholic Church to whom I've pledged my life to Christ. And while what I've been alleged to have viewed might seem embarrassing—we all have our fantasies now don't we—ahem—as I've been hearing—salivating—no, hearing—through your confessions for years now—no?— well, I'm standing here now to inform you—our little invention—our investment will put at risk anyone who does not subscribe. That's right—fail to purchase and you'll risk becoming just like me—having all your fantasies at risk to the world of hackers intent on destroying you, holding you ransom, binding you, keeping you their financial bitch—I mean, I mean prisoner. Yes. Yes. Yes. And do recall that you laity here have far fewer protections than my priesthood affords me. Purchase an ongoing subscription and you will not only be kept safe from those disgusting hackers, you will get to live out every fantasy you've ever dreamed of and then some. And without the dreadful sin of lust. Yessss, that's right. Our little invention bases itself on your unconscious habits, your views, those milliseconds when you should have been scrolling but didn't—<u>not</u> on what you dial in yourself. It's no more sinful than a dream you have in the comfort of your own bed—no sin here when you do not choose it. Right? Rest assured. With your paid subscription, simply turn on HOLY FANTASY before you go to sleep and you will assuredly awaken refreshed, soothed, and, well, in need of a shower.

And it won't harm a soul. No. Not a single one. And you can set that experience to last one minute or hours on end. Imagine it. Yes. Imagine it. The life of every single person improved. Our world made new. Every unknown fantasy lived out without causing any harm to anyone, and no one even needs to know or even be involved. The world used to know this product, this savior, as PURE SMUT. With our investment, PURE SMUT has been rebranded and upgraded with the boldest, newest, anti-hacking technology to become HOLY FANTASY. The very same anti-hacking technology within Ch(e)cker which has kept our campus safe for years now is within HOLY FANTASY. Not a single weapon on this campus for years now. No, no, no. Talk about effective! Talk about bright lines!

With your subscription, you can rest assured that no one—and I mean no one—will ever know <u>your</u> fantasies. And you will be happier letting all of this play out in the background of your life. Your marriages will be stronger—no more sneaking around desiring someone else. Turn on HOLY FANTASY—mind you, after you have done your duty procreating—and you'll never have to worry whether your spouse is cheating on you. Their deeper needs are being taken care of by HOLY FANTASY in the night, just like yours are. In your deepest sleep and theirs. Without you even knowing what it is you are choosing, without having to sift through those messy depths with fruitless years of therapy.

So...my dear world...let us become new creations as our dear Lord Christ invites. I give you HOLY FANTASY. Purchase today and you'll get 10% off the first year with an ongoing subscription checked and selected.

Do yourself a favor—keep yourself safe <u>and</u> live out your every fantasy—you don't even have to select who you want to, uh, who you want in your fantasy and what you want them to do to you and how and even how long. It knows your deeper impulses. It's been studying you for years now, your every view, that extra second where your finger hovered and could've scrolled but didn't, where you lingered, where lust was raging but you were good little boys and girls, though anxiously stifled.

Let HOLY FANTASY take <u>deep</u> care of you. Have only fifteen minutes? Dial it in. Want to fantasize through your eight hours of sleep? Dial it in. I promise you—you will awaken refreshed, alive in the Lord, ready to serve the Lord as you are called to do as teachers, as parents, as fellow clergy. And no mortal sin whatsoever—sin must be chosen for it to really matter. As you well know through the sacramental graces of our most holy church, Christ through his gentle sacramental baptism abolished the disgusting sin of Eve—"

"—uh, nowhere in that story
does it ever say Eve sinned —
and if you actually read the Hebrew story
you would know that it was their genuinely curious
lovemaking, Adam and Eve's hiding themselves in
and around each other,
that made YAHWEH jealous
and that made YAHWEH angry
because YAHWEH was in love with Adam,
the creature YAHWEH first fashioned
from the dirt and breathed into his nose
a blast of life—"

"—and, uh, 'Christ's sacramental baptism'?
Do you not know
that 'baptism' was a drowning ritual?
People—including Jesus—
were supposedly lining up
for the crazy man John—
grasshopper & honey eater—nearly naked—
to dunk them under the dirty water until their last
breath left them—
why? well anyone would have
an experience of new life through that!"

"—the feeling of the wind—of It rushing in!"

"God damn you, women, God damn you to hell for this sinful apostasy—St. Thomas Aquinas sure as hellfire knew Eve had sinned by eating from the Tree of Knowledge—just like St. Augustine knew it—"

"—um, did Augustine even know Hebrew?
Did he? You think he was was able
to catch the clevernesses
of the original Hebrew story
through a translation into Greek,

or even more likely—and even worse—into Latin?"

"Augustine might not have been wrong
about everything
but his attempt at improving
upon Irenaeus' doctrine of original sin
leaves a lot to be desired.
And you'd think that Aquinas
with all his monastic learning
would've explored the Eden story himself
with more care than Augustine—but—"

"Damn you, women, for your sinful theological errors, the Lord damn you Himself to the fires of hell—if you don't subscribe today to HOLY FANTASY you are gone—gone I say—by day's end—secretary, make note of that—gone!—what is it with these disgusting women here—I cannot bear you and if it were all up to me I would have ended the careers of every woman on our faculty—if not for these damned Board-mandated ratios of men-faculty to women-faculty—I'd baptize you in the deep end and then drown you all—but you men, yes you, you are good—better, better than women—but please please please do not eat the fruit that these evil women offer—come to me all you who are tempted and I will refresh you, you and your sons, I will take your heavy burden, yes, come to me and confess to me at any time, and I will refresh you—I will ensure your salvation through the powers invested in me by Christ himself—

HOLY FANTASY. What more can I say? It is a gift to you—my gift to you through the friendship and power of my priesthood—my gift to you all—even you women—but not a free gift. No, no, no, not free. You must buy it, or it buys you and broadcasts your every fantasy to the world as happened to me—well, kind of happened to me as my algorithmic type is surely not financially poor, thin, underage boys with longer hair pulled back in pony tails and wearing wrestling singlets—especially red singlets—that was the hacker—damn it—God damn it—that part was not me—<u>not me</u>—but—but but—

—know your purchase invests in the education of some of the finest students you can imagine here at our college preparatory academy—every purchase helps to fund another underage—I mean student— <u>student</u>—here at St. Thomas Aquinas. Pray for us!

And every purchase helps our faculty and staff gathered here to retire on time—or earlier if possible as their salaries are quite expensive to our overhead and their experience is—quite obviously today—very easily replaceable.

HOLY FANTASY. Plug it into your favorite search engine and know the bliss of life. Subscribe. Try it for only ten minutes if you must—but I practically guarantee you that you will absolutely love it for longer. Much longer.

Remember, purchase today and save—get saved. Don't let lust rule you—instead let your algorithm offer you all the goodness of what it can in the privacy of your own home—instead of being stolen by the hackers to embarrass you into a hell of self-loathing. Subscribe now. Be the hero who saves yourself with the Lord, Christ Himself.

Again, I am yours, Father President Robert Moresley of Saint Thomas Aquinas here in downtown Cincinnati, Ohio. I bid you good day and an even better tonight...with HOLY FANTASY."

0101000 2
2 0001111 232
0000000111110001
323 0000100 2

two voices, interrupted

1. "Jesus—what a meeting, eh? I know the kids will be walking in in a minute or two—probably best they don't see us whispering about it—"

0. "Oh Stan, let's hope they caught the livestreamed version like we did and saw for themselves what a shitty president we have—otherwise all those gaffes have already been edited out and the announcement slimmed down to a tight and perfect fifty seconds or less—where he looks like a fucking genius. That version probably already has a million views by now... maybe two million."

1. "Not the first person to babble on and on to get at least a few usable quotes out of that madness. God help our retirements—and our students' scholarships—especially for the skinny boys Father President so loves—in skin-tight red!"

     Naked Little Fictions: 2029

o. "Jesus, with pony tails. Of course—makes sense now why he doted on Johnny so much. But come on now—be honest, we'll probably be richer—"

1. "You mean our school will be richer—not us. And that's right—you were already subscribed to—what was it called? PURE SMUT?"

o. "Yeah, and you'd probably benefit from the service too. Lord knows, you and Betsy haven't had sex in—what?—fifteen years—"

1. "Twelve. Twelve years. Out of our twenty-four years of marriage. Twelve. Half. Just think, you can be married with kids too—"

o. "Well....I certainly didn't insinuate wanting that...."

1. "Yeah, yeah, yeah, I know. But you could. You could be married—still legal in the country and increasingly accepted by Holy Mother Church. And God knows Father Moresley would never fire you for it, especially when you're, uh, when you're younger."

o. "I don't know, no ponytail here yet. And I prefer wearing blue singlets."

1. "You know you too could come to appreciate the blisses of marriage, and find out what commitment is really about."

o. "Um, hun, in this lust-economy? My kind is smart

enough to marry our best friend so that we can split the mortgage and continue to fuck half the rest of the world—gay or straight."

1. "Half?"

o. "Just the men, honey. Just the men."

1. "Holograms too?"

o. "Depends on how hot they are. HOLY FANTASY for the win!"

1. "I suppose we all have our economies of love. And lust. But not all of them lead to depth or personal growth, now do they, my friend. (*sighs*) Do you really think they could program the President's hologram to answer questions on point for that debate that no one would notice until now—what—six months later? Too suspicious..."

o. "AI works another wonder to behold. Like jacking off to AI porn. From the very same AI innovation our students use to churn out their brilliant theses..."

1. "Did you say 'feces' or 'theses'?"

o. "All too often, about the same, hun."

1. "At least you and I aren't using AI to grade their all too often terrible AI-written papers. How many of our colleagues churn out their pages and pages

of AI-driveled feedback for our students to improve their papers...?"

0. "Loopty loops of wisdom...."

1. "Moresely getting his algorithm leaked last year—and now using that to scare us into subscribing—basically investing in our own retirements—think that's any coincidence or just a good save?"

0. "Dunno."

1. "Why do you think he did it—Moresley? Why invest our entire portfolio in HOLY FANTASY?"

0. "'*Vaulting ambition*,' don't you think? Probably wants to be named a Cardinal, a red-robed prince of the church."

1. "Well, we all know how such ambitions play out."

0. "Here comes Aro. I've been worried about him. Better go and try to connect."

1. "Good luck on that one. Pink hair today. Wow. Bold move with today's field trip dress code of coat and tie."

0. "Aro. Aro! Aro, hello—I see you don't have your buds in. You can hear me."

1. "Aro—we, uh, we saw your dad this morning—"

"Gross."

0. "Um, okay, well. I'm sure he's, I'm sure he's proud of you—good talking, Stan—see you at the front steps at 9:00—um, Aro, um I like what you've done with your, with your hair—"

"Wha—"

0. "Good morning, good morning, exciting day, everyone, yep, come on in, good morning, good morning. Play Day! Good morning, Patrick—"

"Oh—my—fucking—God— the faggot has pink hair now—"

0. "Patrick! Patrick, not only did you say the wrong thing that will earn you detention for another week—at least—but you said it so loudly and didn't know that you did because you have your buds in—"

"You think I didn't hear myself?
Now <u>that</u>'s funny. A detention?
What? On Father President's big day?
What would my good uncle—Daddy Dearest—
Father President—
Great-Uncle Bobby—at least to me—
what would he have to say about that—
I mean, I think I'm speaking in turn, right—
President's great-nephew outranks

Vice Chair's pink-haired son-or-whatever outranks
measly high school English teacher, right?
Am I right, everyone?
You all know I'm right.
How's our cheer go?
'That's alright, that's okay,
you're gonna work for me someday...hey hey!'"

o. "—Patrick, take your seat, Patrick, and your buds,
take your buds out so you can hear me—"

"—am I in your fantasy-deck
on PURE SMUT, Mr. Fag—?"

o. "—Patrick, that's quite enough—unless you
want to spend the rest of the year in detention—
and you heard your Great Uncle—Father President
Moresley—it's now HOLY FANTASY—"

"—better lock down that ongoing subscription
to PURE SMUT or whatever he's calling it now,
better have it paid to perpetual <u>ON</u>, Mr. Fagiole,
or else the whole world's gonna know
just how much you've been lusting after me—
all those looksies on my socials—
have I sent you my nudes yet?"

o. "Patrick! Take your buds out this instant so you
can hear how many detentions I'm entering in your
name—"

"—Mr. Fagiole, can we please talk
about something worthwhile.
Patrick is such a douche—"

"—oh hun, I can smell ya from here—"

o. "—thank you for that segway, Madeleine, we do indeed need to read the exciting conclusion to *Macbeth* before we meet the other classes on the front steps to walk to the theatre. So please get out your *Macbeth* and let's have a dramatic reading of Act V so we know where it's all heading before we soon see Act I onstage. Madeleine, could you please read the part of Gentlewoman, and, um, Aro—"

"—Pink!"

o. "—Aro, could you please read for Doctor?"

"Fuck nah."

0101121011

23232323232323230101112323232

same two voices, interrupted by a sea of voices

o. "Stan, we'll be safe here, right—with that protest over there and all—"

1. "On Fountain Square? Of course. Ch(e)cker. You heard our most dear Father President bragging all about it."

o. "Well, the only reason I bring it up is that Aro had to check his knife at the Square entryway—"

1. "—whaaat?! When did he get a knife?! At the play?!"

o. "Had to be somewhere between school and here—must've had it delivered."

1. "Delivered? But we've been with him—"

o. "You know, by drone."

1. "Jesus. There's too much to keep track of anymore. He's weaponless now, right?"

0. "I guess. Ch(e)cker let him onto the Square....?"

1. "Yeah. Probably better keep an eye on him. The headlines on that one would be bad news on our watch. VICE-CHAIR'S SON SLAYS HOMOPHOBIC PRESIDENT'S GREAT-NEPHEW BELOW FOUNTAIN SQUARE'S GENIUS OF WATERS, TEACHERS SMILE PROUDLY AND APPLAUD."

0. "Hilarious. (*sighs*) Hard to imagine any age with geniuses...."

1. "Hey bud, our bud Willy Shakes lives. *'Yet who would have thought the old man to have had so much blood in him?'*"

0. "*'Do you mark that?'* (*laughs*) Bravo! Good show! We both know this one too well."

1. "Well, I've taught **Macbeth** twenty-five years now. Even your three years teaching it is nothing to snuff at."

0. "Umhmm."

1. "With all that wisdom from the past, you'd think we'd be able to solve our country's problems by now. Or at least our school's."

0. "Jesus, come on, Stan—"

1. "—same game being played over and over again—in every generation a new blue-blooded idiot with '*vaulting ambition*' and people rally around him without question to get their share of the spoils—and most of it essentially stolen from those with less buying power."

0. "You got a better idea? I'd vote for you as Father President—"

1. "—instead of all of us doing the very hard work of figuring it out together as equals."

0. "What do you mean?"

1. "I mean, think back to Act V: Malcolm has the head of dead king Macbeth there in his hands—the head of the king who killed a king to claim the throne—and what does Malcolm do? He enacts the very same system that killed the beloved king before him—allows himself to be crowned king and hands out promotions to a ring of sycophants who will do his royal bidding to grow their own wealth and prestige. For Chris'sake! Could we finally do something new?!"

0. "Gotta put up with Moresley's blue-balled bullshit to get our paychecks and retirements...."

1. "That's exactly it—that's exactly the problem as I see it. We continue to add our yesses to the systems we've inherited—systems that are killing us

at the hands of some power-drunk boyish fool who knows how to manipulate the system to his own ends. Systems that double-bind us—that make us stay for the love or security and meanwhile kill us slowly."

0. "It's not just the boys playing these games. You remember the way Harriet ran our department two years ago—"

1. "Truth. (sighs) I mean, who knows, maybe a senate of faculty and board members would come to the same decision as Moresley did—invest in Ch(e)cker or HOLY FANTASY or whatever. Who knows. But at least it would be a decision that we all came to and had to live with and not just living under his rule, his deciding for us—and often to advance his own cause, his own position."

0. "Cardinal Moresley. We knew him when...."

1. "Our school—our country—our time—we're tormented—*'troubled with thick-coming fancies That keep her from her rest.'*"

0. "Sounds like my dates lately..."

1. "Hard to know if this political situation we're all in—school and country, sadly—is like the marriage we're meant to stick out for our own personal growth or the marriage you must leave to save your life."

0. "Leave...?"

1. "I guess we could leave—but—"

0. "Not so easy. Easier for me than you. But still not so easy for any of us."

1. "Swimming away from shipwrecks—with too many fucking splinters everywhere."

0. "Well, what do you really make of last night's revelation—the whole hologram business?"

1. "Oh I don't know. At least they programmed him to say the same ridiculously unclever things he usually does."

0. "I guess if they do it to Whitney and people will pay to see her likeness on stage, then they can do it for the President of the United States so that he can attend his son's grade school basketball game in peace."

1. "Wonder what kind of costume he wore at the game—"

0. "—with all those Secret Service dressed up too?!"

1. "The tough thing for me is that he and his ring agreed—committed—to the debate dates—you know—ahead of time—and his whole campaign to restore decency and democracy and decorum—and then they go pull this stunt—"

0.	"Stan, should we uh—the protestors over there—"

1.	"Hey—hey—Aquinas students—get away from that group over there! Stay over on this side—"

0.	"I think you mean 'groups'...but hey should we just leave, head back?"

1.	"You heard Father President...we're as safe here as at school...."

— unsure laughter from both —

0.	"Jesus, would you look at that—what's Patrick—"

1.	"Oh—he's just not-so-heterosexually appreciating our erotic fountain—our Genius and her naked sea-creature-wrestling masculine minions—"

0.	"—running his fingers over—Jesus—over their naked legs—Jeessssus—who's the gay one now—"

1.	"The Genius of Waters takes all comers. Here in the Queen City with her gay-haters and gay-minions alike. Truly alike. Like I said—same games no matter the political party, no matter the century. Religionists and the Whatever-We-Call-What's-Left, same games."

0.	"Is that a snake there—in that sculpture's hand?"

1. "And a rock in the other hand—to smash the snake, we might surmise. Yes. Right where the water gushes out—right where Patrick is—is—"

0. "Oh—my—God—"

1. "Too much for this oldish straight guy."

0. "We'll let your personal algorithm be the judge of that. Better get that PURE SMUT—HOLY FANTASY, HOLY FANTASY—boost your ever-looming retirement—get that subscription on monthly renewal to make sure none of us ever knows just how uninterested you are by Patrick's accidentally squirting water everywhere, haha."

1. "Yeah, wouldn't want any of my daydreams of retirement in twenty more very long years leaking out into the world too early, for sure—damnit, this protest is cramping our free-time style."

0. ***"The cry is still 'They come!'"***

1. "Yeahhh. I really don't want to get us back to the classroom too early—"

"Demofools, Demofools, go get screwed!"

"Religionists kill, Religionists lie, Religionists—die!"

1. "Do you think Patrick even knows they're so close to him? His damned buds in again. We better get him away from there—"

0. "And why is Aro—why is Aro sneaking up behind Patrick—shittttt—"

"Demofools, Demofools, go get screwed!"

"Religionists kill, Religionists lie, Religionists—die!"

0. "Stan, grab him! Aro—don't you dare—get away—get away from Patrick—"

— *lightening strike* —

— *exceedingly heavy rain splattering* —

— *for minutes* —

...once it's clear enough to see...

0. "Stan, Stan, what the hell—"

1. "Patrick, Patrick, put your clothes back on—what did you—"

o. "Stan, Aro—Aro's naked—Aro's naked—there on the ground—Aro's nnn—Aro—Aro—what—"

"What's with these three boys
on the ground all naked
—what the fu—"

o. "Three?"

"Three—look there—
those two kids and that other one—
he looks like that statue from the fountain—
what the hell—"

o. "Stan, Stan—are you alright? Stan—Stan—did the lightening—"

"Their clothes on the ground there—
like they did it themselves—
look—took them off by themselves—"

"One of them there sure looks like
them fountain boys—"

"And now that girl over there is naked—"

o. "Madeleine! No!"

"Oh yesss, Mr. Fagiole—yessss—"

"And that Religionist over there—why—why—
he's taking off his shirt—"

"And his pants—"

"And —and—uh—
his underwear—and—"

"And that guy he was heckling—just before the
storm started—and they look drunk or high--"

"And that old lady over there too—
Jesus—what the—"

o. "Stan—Stan—is that a snake swallowing its own
tail—Stan—Stan—are you paying attention—Stan—
what does that mean again, Stan?"

"—that snake—it's getting away—"

"—where'd that snake come from?"

"But they're not even touching each other—
none of them naked people
on the ground are even touching—"

"—yeah—that's the strangest thing—
all of them there writhing on the ground there—
I always thought nakedness meant sex—"

"—but obviously not here—
they're nowhere near each other—"

"—and not even touching themselves really—"

"—but they're slithering, writhing on the ground—
I mean, look at their faces—
that's not pain—
it's like—like—like they're in—in—"

"—ecstasy—"

"—they look like those paintings of the saints
when they're in deep—"

"—deep union—"

"—Jesus—"

"—ecstasy—"

"—but why them—why not us—"

"—in ecstasy—"

0. "Stan—don't touch—you shouldn't reach out to him when he's na—"

1. "Patrick, Patrick, are you okay, son—"

0. "Stan—stop—are you alright? You look—woozy. Stan, Stan, don't get any nearer to him—to them— Stan—Stan—no—<u>no</u>, Stan—stop—Stan—you can't take your clothes off here—the kids, Stan—STOP— the kids!"

1. "—oh my God—oh my God—it feels—so—ah—yes—oh God—so good—fuck—"

0. "Stan—Stan—well, at least you're not touching them—okay—okay—it will be okay—okay—Father President—he'll—he'll make it right—"

1. "—God, come on, you—you'll love it—fuck—you'll love it—just—just lean in—yes—that sound—the wind—feel the sound—feel the sound on your skin—It leads you—just let It touch you—yesss—God—"

0. "Feel the sound—what are—? Touch—me?! What—Stan—what?"

1. "The breeze—God—here—"

2.

inspiration

Once. In a fiction. Told long, long ago. As a warning.

The people asked for a king.

They asked for a king—and they got Saul, whose name means 'they asked for it.'

Saul had some early successes unifying the people of his nation—but soon he started doing things only for himself and his own benefit, like building penis-statues in his honor for sex-themed parties he'd host.

As a king, Saul was a christ, an oil-smeared one...the first king/christ of his nation in this fictional story. King Saul went up against the enemy-Philistines but shrank from Goliath's challenge and sent the boy David out to fight Goliath instead of himself. In that challenge-match alone, Saul demonstrated he was no person of honor—to send a boy out against a giant!!

After that, some of Saul's women-subjects used to make fun of Saul by singing a catchy little jingle to his face: "Saul kills his thousand; David kills his millions."

That jingle infuriated Saul so much that his royal

attendants (slaves) sought a boy (slave) to soothe Saul by strumming Saul's strings. They fetched David, who had killed the enemy-giant Goliath, to be this balm for their king and bring the king out of his bad moods.

Christ Saul fell in love with the youngster-boy David but later wanted to kill the boy, tried to pin David to the wall with his spear, his kingly prerogative as christ, as oil-smeared king.

David ran away to Samuel, the one who reluctantly gave the people what they wanted by anointing/ christening Saul king. Samuel knew that when the people demanded a king rule over them like all the other nations that the people had rejected YAHWEH as their king of life, of the breeze that enlivens all life. As an ecstatic/prophet, Samuel served the breeze— YAHWEH—alone.

Saul sent three battalions of his own troops to fetch David and bring him back so that he could kill David and put an end to the madness the Goliath-killing youngster stirred up in him. But each battalion fell to the ground in ecstasy in front of Samuel and couldn't do what the king demanded of them. So Saul decided to go himself, to fetch David, to kill David himself.

David's name means 'the one who boils over with affection'....something most translations don't tell you...deeper meaning that becomes so obvious in the words and even stylish sounds of the original Hebrew stories...

**a more honest translation of the Bible,
1 Samuel 19, beginning at verse 22:**

And when Saul had arrived—
  he'd gone all the way to the great well
  which is at that sharp-place where only thorns grow,
  where wild phenomena happen,
  where all can be observed it's so high—

he asked—(Saul, the king named 'they asked for it')—
he said,
"Where are Samuel and David?"

And someone said,
"Listen up here—
in the shepherds' pen in The Heights."

And he went there—
to the shepherds' pen in The Heights—

  and It was upon him— even him!—
  the divine wind was—

and he went, went, went—did he ever go!—

and became ecstatic as prophets do—
  all the way until (fuck) he entered into the
  shepherds' pen in The Heights—

and he stripped himself of his clothes—spread himself
out and flailed around—

even he did!—
and became ecstatic—
even he did!—
right there in front of Samuel's face—
and he fell down naked-and-sly
all day and all night...

and that's why they say,
   "Is even Saul among the ecstatics?!"

Read any English translation of 1 Samuel 19:22-24 and you'll see similar elements as above—including the naked-prophet motif. But rarely do all of these stylish elements appear in most Bible translations from the Hebrew.

The Naked Path of Prophet *and* **Ecstatic Prophets, Compulsive Fascists**—*these newest translations of 1 Samuel warn about the dangers of kings and christs and organized religion...and instead invite readers to the ecstatic style and lifestyle in the big breeze...the ecstatic, clever style of living with YAHWEH, king of the breezes, king of all life...*

YAHWEH
...honored by these ecstatics...these prophets...
styling it out ever naked and ever sly
with their wild stories...

(in Hebrew, 'naked' and 'sly' have the exact same letters,
just stressed differently when spoken aloud)

these mountain-dwelling ecstatics
living on the edge of empires intent on attempting
to control life/nature,

these laughter-inspiring ecstatics
sounding it out differently, noticing, feeling,
knowing through spine-tingling experience
how the wind transforms
even bloodthirsty enemies into fellow ecstatics...

and you too?

about the author

In addition to **The Naked Path of Prophet** series, Brian Shircliff is the poet of **winds of (r)evolution** (paintings by Matthew Klooster) and author of the graphic novel **YAHWEH IS THE WIND!** (illustrated by Sean K. Long). Having taught high school religion for seventeen years, he felt the need to swim away from the shipwreck of organized religion for a more inclusive perspective. He is a Bones for Life® Trainer, Guild Certified Feldenkrais Practitioner®, Healing Touch Certified Practitioner, and thirty-year student of many styles of meditation, tai chi, and yoga. He co-founded and continues to direct VITALITY Cincinnati's donation-based holistic self-care programs.

about the artist

Julie Lucas designed this book's cover with a photo of the Tyler Davidson Fountain taken by Brian Shircliff, her Adobe Stock images, and her own artistry. Julie is a graphic designer, illustrator and meditator whose creative process draws from inquiry and deep listening into the heart of it all. Her first creative project with VITALITY was designing our logos, and since then nearly every book cover we've published. See more of her work at **withinwonder.com**.

* bold-italicized quotes in the novella are from *Macbeth*

about VITALITY

VITALITY is a circle of friends welcoming all, awakening each other, and reminding each other that we are Whole.

Our affordable self-care programs invite everyone to move, to breathe, to rest, to contemplate, to grow... wherever each person begins their self-care journey, wherever and however they want to become.

It's the power of a circle!

We invite you to explore with us

through our donation-based drop-in classes...
in person & via Zoom

affordable trainings

individual sessions

volunteer opportunities

vitalitycincinnati.org

publishing books from VITALITY's circle of friends
inspiring love, creativity, + possibility

vitalitybuzz.org